max
and
moonbean

For Lucas, Zachary, and Isabella
and the friendships you make
—R.S.

Max and Moonbean
Copyright © 2023 by Robert Scotton
All rights reserved. Manufactured in Italy.
No part of this book may be used or reproduced in any manner whatsoever without written permission
except in the case of brief quotations embodied in critical articles and reviews. For information address
HarperCollins Children's Books, a division of HarperCollins Publishers, 195 Broadway, New York, NY 10007.
www.harpercollinschildrens.com

Library of Congress Control Number: 2022941733
ISBN 978-0-06-299038-9

The artist used Photoshop and Painter on iMac Pro to create the illustrations for this book.
Typography by Rick Farley
23 24 25 26 27 RTLO 10 9 8 7 6 5 4 3 2 1
First Edition

max and moonbean

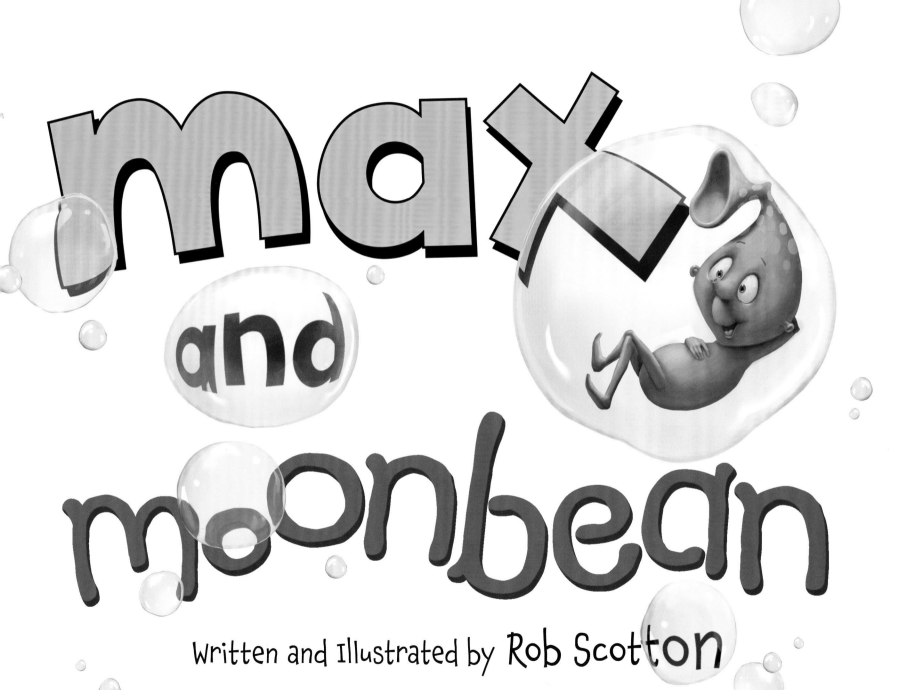

Written and Illustrated by Rob Scotton

HARPER
An Imprint of HarperCollinsPublishers

Max twiddled his fingers
And tapped his toes
As he nervously waited his turn
For show-and-tell.

"Why do my show-and-tells never go well?" Max wondered aloud. "Dare to see what you can do," replied a little voice.

"Your turn, Max," said Mr. Whisker, the teacher.

Max took a deep breath and began.
"Last night, I boggled my brain looking for
A fun thing for show-and-tell.

"I searched in my closet
And around my bed.
I looked under my fish
And behind Mr. Ted."

"But I found nothing,
And show-and-tell loomed.
Without a fun story
I was doomed.

"So I asked my shadow:
'What should I do?'
My shadow just shrugged.
It hadn't a clue."

"A flash caught my eye,
And through the window, afar,
I spied a light in the sky,
A bright shooting star.

"Through the window it blazed
Like a furious rocket.
It spun me around
And crashed in my closet."

"And when the dust cleared
I was shocked to see
A strange blue thingy
Staring at me."

"I wanted to hide
But stood strong all the same.
I bravely stepped forward
And asked, 'What's your name?'

"The blue thingy smiled
With a slightly odd stare
And a bubble, then two
Popped into the air."

"A moon and a bean,
Then followed a thought:
Moonbean was the name
Of this blue astronaut.

"'Where did you come from
To be here in my room?'
Moonbean raised a finger
That led to the moon."

"'Max,' Moonbean said,
'You're funny and swell.
Will you come to the moon
To be my show-and-tell?'

"'I don't think I can.
You see, I'm really quite shy.'
'Pifaffle!' said Moonbean.
'You're a can-do guy.'"

"'You're a pup of courage,
Clever and kind,

Of impeccable style

And squeaky behind.'

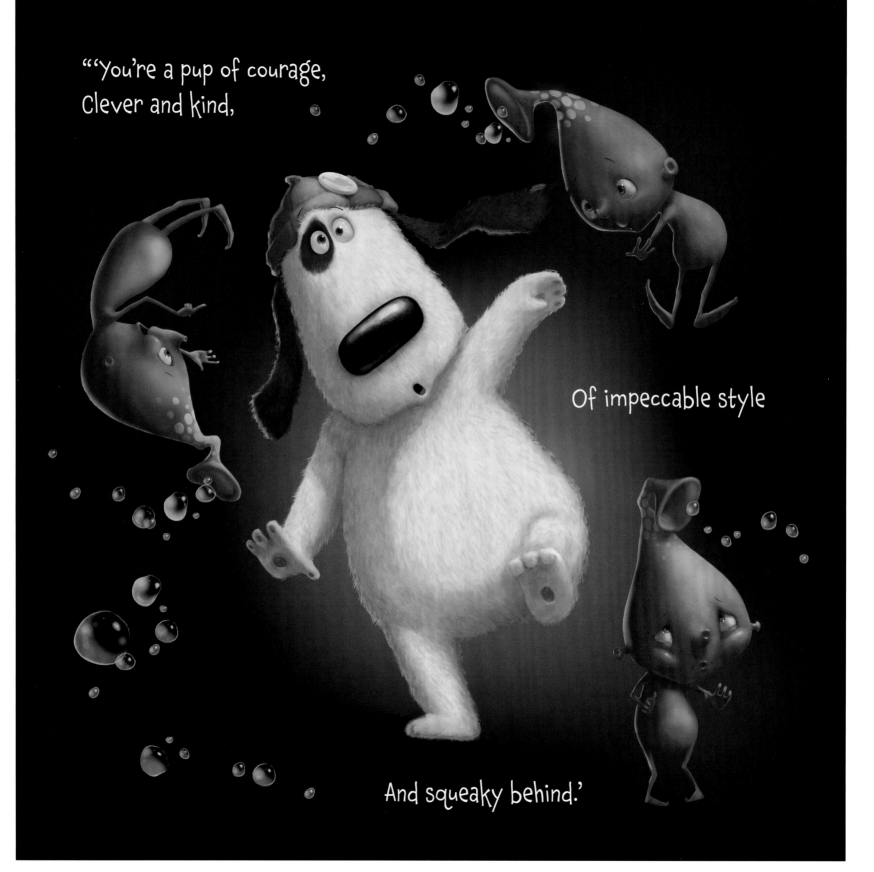

"We spoke of adventures to come
And the wonders we'd see.
Then we sped into space,
My blue friend and me."

"We flew fast and high
Past planets and stars.

I oohed at Saturn

And aahed at Mars."

"I looked back at our world
A planet so small,
A beautiful, precious,
Fragile blue ball."

"Then on to the moon
I was a show-and-tell hit.
And to my surprise
Not nervous one bit.

"As we set off for home
I waved my farewell.
Then I asked Moonbean,
'Will you be my show-and-tell?'"

"'Of course!' Moonbean said.
'Let's do it. Let's go.
You're sure to be
The star of the show.'

"We're Moonbean and Max,
Friends through and through.
Let's dare to see
What we can do."

"And that's my story.
And this is . . . Moonbean!"
But Moonbean wasn't in the box.

Instead, a single bubble rose into the air.

It grew bigger . . .

and bigger . . .

until . . .

It popped.

"That was spectacular!"
cried Mr. Whisker.
"Well done, Max."
The class cheered.
Max was thrilled.

But later, Max was confused.

Very confused.

Where did Moonbean go?
The answer was a tap, tap, tap away.

"I was beside you the whole time," Moonbean said.
"You couldn't see me,
But I could see you.
And you were amazing.

"Sometimes it takes a friend to show us how amazing we really are."

"We're Moonbean and Max,
Friends through and through.
Let's dare to see
What we can do."